LOST PIECES: PART I

AVIN PRAKASH

ISBN 979-888569750-7

To and For my Father, my first novelette

Contents

Prologue

Marshal Max Mellow was currently pretty bored of his job in the USA.

Being an original English inhabitant, he had faced a hell lot of crimes in his area, and the peace this place had was not just boring... it was unnerving. Also, he hated being nicknamed. And 'the chief wasn't even a proper nickname.

He sighed. His promotion was no better than three demotions.

Suddenly, the landline in front of him rang.

Finally, he thought.

"Marshal Mellow," the caller said, "How dear to you is your life?"

"Very much?"

"Oh... that's good. You don't sound like an ideal policeman."

Mellow chuckled, "Think again."

"There is no need," the caller's voice sounded strangely monotone.

"Okay. Go on. Threaten me."

The caller sounded vaguely amused. "Someone's calling."

And that exact moment, the chief's phone rang.

Horrified, he looked at it. It was Seren, his daughter. No matter what happened, he never declined her call.

He picked the call, "What happened Seren?"

"Hi Mellow," it was the previous caller's voice. "Seems like the three minutes isn't enough. Nothing will be."

ONE

Expensive Keys

Richie woke up early, as he planned with his friends.

And today, he again had to do some tough task that was really easy for him. He ran to the restroom, got fresh and then went straight for his cycling helmet as silently as he could. But his mother was used to this silence so she was easily able to figure out something moving even when she was half asleep.

"Where are you going, Richard?"

"Early morning cycling!" he replied.

"Um okay," she said with a yawn.

"Where?" his father said with not even a hint of sleep in his tone.

"Around... Mr Starbuck's house!"

Before his father could say anything, his mother cut him. "You two just LET me sleep. I do NOT sleep the whole day like you two."

"Sure mom!" he said and ran off, leaving his father yelling behind.

He grabbed his cycle, "That was easy," he said to himself.

"Surely it was," Chris said, coming to a stop with a nice stunt. "Everyone's groggy in the morning."

"It's foggy. Isn't it?" Richie asked.

"No problem for me," Chris said.

Richie smiled at him, "I will ask that question in hell from you after you are caught trespassing."

"Thanks for the good wishes," he grunted and started off at full speed.

"Hey, I was just kidding, wait!" Richie said, laughing really hard.

His yard was full of snow and only the space cleaned by his father was there for him to pass. Plus, the ground was frozen and wet, so he was using his customized cycle. It was easy to drive it. Currently, his cycle was cutting straight through the snow. He took a right turn and headed behind Chris, between bare trees to the Grande house.

The day before yesterday, Chris has (by mistake) slipped Reigh's cycle lock keys down the back gate of the Grande hall (the house of the previous mayor who died a week ago due to some genetic disease), and now it was his job to bring it back.

They turned straight into just one clear path of the forest land visible. After cycling on the forest floor for 5 minutes, they turned in into their base, The Christone, a tent set up which was guarded by a treehouse just above it. Just to tease Chris, it was named that way, but now they called it Christone only. It was grand by their standards since it had all the camper's necessities, ranging from pen knife to maps to food. It was where they played and talked usually. Their parents didn't know about this place and they decided they will never let them.

Reigh just sat on the top of their treehouse, dangling his legs down. He was absolutely ready.

He jumped down the ladder and then climbed down the other set.

"I am only getting you the keys, Chris," he said and walked beside them.

"Don't you think he acts as if he's the best," Chris said.

Richie rolled his eyes. "C'mon."

"Yeah yeah favour him," he said.

"Hey I never said anything!" he said, trying to catch up with Reigh and Chris.

"Three teams," Reigh said at the gates. "You guys have your phones right?"

"Have you ever seen them away from us?" Richie asked.

"Well, yeah... no."

"Go on."

"I will grab the keys of the back gate, and I will need Richie. We will get it to Chris, who will get in and grab the keys, and may I specify ONLY THE KEYS, and get away."

"Of course," Chris said.

"One second," Richie said, "Three teams, right?"

Reigh scoffed, "You will have only three minutes to get the keys. Not even a second more than that. Because otherwise, I will cut the line."

"Oh hell, you are not involving *her* right?" Chris asked.

"We have only one option, and that's *her*. I will get the keys." And he cycled away. Chris looked at Richie, his mouth half-open. Richie just shrugged and followed Reigh.

Reigh took off his jacket and placed it neatly over his cycle. Then he parked his cycle at one of the edges of the Grande hall.

The first disadvantage is that the walls were completely straight, so anyone and everyone can look at you coming, and then you are murdered.

The second disadvantage, the walls were perfectly smooth with the top barbed.

The third disadvantage, the walls were just *HUGE.* And that was a *HUGE* disadvantage. That is why Reigh involved Seren in all this.

And the fourth disadvantage, the guard.

An armed guard in black was always standing there, and the key is inside the belt loop of his pants. Reigh smiled and went to the coffee shop across the street. It has opened early, like always. He went inside. "I have come to take the guard's coffee," he said.

Usually, the guard sent a homeless person or anyone passing that way to get him a cup of hard black coffee, and in return, he gave a bit of extra money to that person. A kid without a jacket in the bitter cold- who would do better?

The shopkeeper made a cup of coffee and brought it to him.

Reigh placed double money on the table. "One more cup."

The shopkeeper grunted but made one more. After all, he was getting money for his work.

"Thanks," Reigh said and walked off. He threw off his scarf and wore a face mask, his jacket and a cap on top on his way to the guard.

He smiled as he saw the guard, who looked like a mean and rare bad bald guy.

"Your coffee sir," he said, "The shopkeeper has a special deal of buy one get one free today because of black Friday, and he has sent you coffee! He'll charge money though for one."

"Thanks," he said as Reigh handed him two cups and the gun he was holding almost fell, which he rested against his leg, and Reigh made him hold the coffee.

Then Reigh showed his palm, but the guard was not able to move, balancing the AK-47 with one leg and two steaming cups of coffee with his hands.

"Can you... just pull out my wallet? Currently, it has only as much money as you need. Then just keep the wallet on the ground."

He beamed. The guard also smiled and nodded. Reigh took the wallet and then took the money. He placed the wallet casually on the floor after taking the money and then nodded and walked off.

After he was at a safe distance from the guard, he smiled at the keys, glittering in his hands.

He cycled to Chris and handed him the keys.

The trick was the simplest one. He had a small but sharp paper cutter with which he slashed the loop of his belt and *Voila!* he got the keys.

"Where's Richie?" Chris asked.

Reigh smiled the most amused smile of the day. "Doing his part."

Richie constantly inhaled and exhaled in front of the colonel's house. "You can do it," he told himself, "You can do it, you can do it," and then he knocked, by mistake almost breaking the door.

"Yes?" Seren's mother answered.

"I witnessed a theft!" he yelled on the top of his voice. "I need to see the chief!"

"You are not joking?" she asked.

"You can check."

She nodded grimly, "Come in."

Reigh called with Chris on a call conference.

"I cannot believe your trick worked. How much time do you need?" Seren asked.

"You have only three minutes, right?"

"Before my dad knows. Yup. My phone is on tag especially when you call."

"Hey!" Reigh complained. "I am no criminal."

She laughed "You just proved your point."

"You have very little time!" Richie's voice came over the phone.

"Richie can act real nice huh?"

"Thanks for the tea! But the guard is in DANGER!" Richie said.

"Yeah, got your point, Richie. Enter, Chris."

"You have nice earphones," the colonel said. "Where did you buy them from?"

"Can we speak about this later?"

"Sure sure. Where were we?"

"At your house?"

"What's the position?" Reigh asked.

"Just open the locks first," Seren said.

The only reason why there was no guard on that door was the huge lock that when opened sent a notification to the guard's phone.

And Reigh was opening that door only.

"Can we do it a bit more peaceful, without involving my father and all?" Seren asked.

"Nope," Reigh said.

"You sure he will never catch you?"

Reigh took out his jacket, pulled out the sleeves, and then wore it again.

"Oh nice," Seren said.

He turned the key and the alarms went off.

Reigh again wore his jacket the other way and walked off towards the main gate.

The guard was coming towards him. Reigh walked beside him, brushing his shoulder with the guard. The guard turned and looked at him for a while. Then his eyes widened and he yelled behind Reigh "STOP!"

But Reigh continued walking.

He came in front of the main gate. One of the cups of coffee was still there. He dropped the keys inside the coffee and then started running.

“Inside the coffee,” he spoke on his phone.

“Fine,” Seren said. “I am tracking you guys. Chris now’s your chance. Start walking.”

“I cannot keep him following me for long,” Reigh said.

“And I can hear muffled speaking of my dad with someone. I guess the guard reported.” Seren said.

“Guys I am running as naturally as I can,” Chris said.

“Seren, guide me,” Reigh said.

“Let me see,” she tapped a few commands on her laptop. “Turn the next right.”

He followed her command and the guard followed him.

“Left,” she said.

“Okay.”

“How close is the guard?” she asked.

“About 50 feet,” he said, panting.

“You are good to go. Turn the next left and jump straight into my grandmother’s house,” she said.

Reigh whistled. “Intelligent.”

“Thank you.”

"By the way," Reigh said, "I thought that your grandmother lived in London."

She winked, "There are a lot of things you do not know about me."

“I am in,” Chris said.

“Nice. Now get his keys,” Seren said.

“I have seen it. Now I am running towards it... And...”

He abruptly stopped.

At his right, there was a single floored Chinese house, made completely of wood. It was glossy and shiny, and it looked beautiful. But that was not which caught his attention. It was the centrepiece of a table, which was clearly visible because of the open sliding door.

He felt attracted to it. His feet slid between the grass floor and he walked towards it.

"Chris!" Reigh was yelling.

He had lost concentration looking at it. He came to his senses and ran towards Reigh's keys and slid out through the back door.

The next day, all the news flashed the same thing: '*Lost and found seeking thief! Mysterious thief who stole a bunch of cycle keys! The greatest lost keys in American history."*

"So we got our keys and made it to the news," Reigh said.

"*Your* keys," Chris corrected.

"But what if they caught you two? Chris, you did not take anything, did you?" Richie asked.

"Well, I did find something nice," he confessed.

"The thing that matters, you didn't take it right?" Reigh asked

"Well..." then he noticed the glares from Richie and Reigh "I didn't take anything! I am just telling you two. Trust me."

"What was so special that you saw?"

"A golden Rubik's cube with no other colour. It was completely golden. There was not even a single colour except golden."

"What makes it so special?" Reigh asked, suddenly sounding interested.

"Without colours, what is the use of a Rubik's cube? That is why it seemed pretty strange."

"Reigh," Richie said, "Stop dreaming. You are not getting it in your lifetime." He sat back and made himself comfortable at the old sofa they somehow conjured for the Christone.

"Yeah," Reigh said with a sigh. "You are right."

"Let's go now. I have my debate tomorrow and I have a huge speech to prepare." Richie said.

"Okay, so meet you guys later," Chris said.

They both left with their bicycle, leaving Reigh alone.

Suddenly his phone rang after an hour.

Night ten O'clock. Who would be calling?

He picked up the caller. And his face turned pale in fifteen seconds.

Reigh locked himself inside Christone after he looked at the number. It was his own.

He immediately called Chris.

"Yeah?"

"That golden cube. You took it."

"No, I didn't."

"This NOT a question this is a statement and I just received a death threat."

"Come on. Now you are making it up. I got your keys, that's all."

"No, I am not." A second later, he added, "Where are you?"

"At my home."

"Change your location turn off GPS *now.*"

"That's easy."

"Do it."

"Done."

"Now run."

He went out of his door. "Where to?"

"To Christone. Fast."

But Chris missed one thing important.

He didn't notice the movement behind him.

"Be quick!" Reigh said.

"I am being quick," he said considering all this a joke.

A shadow closed in towards him...

Chris' mother called him from behind, "Chris!"

"Yes mom!" he replied.

"Run!" Reigh yelled again.

A spine shaking howl shook the very foundations of Reigh's brain.

We slapped the phone shut and started to breathe heavily.

The words of the caller were simple:

"This is Superior executing agent Franklin Ross. You have something that belongs to me. I have some people looking after you. They can easily kill you anytime you wish. Just tell them. But do as they tell you. My men will contact you soon. I have easily observed that you have a lot of brains, but soon your dead body will not be needing it. I need the healing agent."

Reigh's keys have cost Chris his life.

And the strangest thing?

Franklin Ross was the most renowned scientist in his town.

And Ross was in the field of genetic engineering.

TWO
SO-CALLED CRIMINAL

Seren was tired of trying to reach Reigh's phone.

"That's rare," she said to herself, "Reigh always answers immediately."

"Is it so?" a voice said behind her.

She turned, blushing, "Umm... dad..."

"I have removed your three minutes limit," he said, taking a chair and sitting on it. "You can talk to him as long as you wish."

"Dad..."

"Shh," he said, "I am your father. I can limit you and take your limits. I was only worried that you would not have been safe outside the house. I have a lot of enemies out there." He looked at the windows.

Seren held his hands, "Dad nothing will happen to me. Your enemies are nothing against me. Also, I thought you were bored because you *did not* have enemies."

Her father laughed. "By the way, what's with Reigh?"

"Umm... well..."

"I know what you did yesterday. Getting cycle keys is not a crime."

"If you already know that, what are you asking?"

"Well..." he was cut off by the sudden ringing of Seren's phone.

Her father indicated her to give him the phone with a hint of humour lightning his face. She smiled and handed him her phone.

He picked the caller and his face too turned pale.

Seren saw the change in colour. "Dad?"

Her dad hung up the caller. He looked at the phone for a while. Then he slowly held forward her phone.

"Don't tell me he's in trouble."

"He is. You are. Those two also are. I am too. And this trouble is really hard to get rid of."

"Dad, you solve murder mysteries in a day. But Reigh wouldn't have called for reporting a case, would he have?"

"It wasn't him. And Chris most probably is almost dead. I cannot tell you more. We all are in trouble. And you and Reigh can get us out of this."

"What's the problem in telling me?"

"He is everywhere."

Seren shook her head and narrowed her eyes.

Her father said only three words after that, kissed her forehead, and leaving her mystified, he left the room. She sensed that she was not seeing him again for a long time.

And her instincts were true.

Seren's phone rang again. She looked at the caller.

"Richie what's happening?" she asked.

"Where's Reigh?" He asked on the phone.

"I... I dunno."

"We all are in trouble."

"I know that."

"You do? Do you know that tons of blood have been found in front of Chris' house?"

"Nice hyperbole."

She could sense him rolling his eyes. "Okay, huge quantity of blood. I am sending you the picture. But it's some sort of prank. I am pretty sure."

"He messaged you himself?"

"Yes... oh, here comes one more."

"What does it say?" she asked.

"You will be called to witness this you would say it is done by... WHAT? THIS IS HELL INSANE!"

"What happened?" she asked.

"It says you are supposed to say... you witnessed Reigh trying to kill him. Do not try to change your statement or the same will happen to you." He scoffed. "Someone tell him his pranks are boring."

Suddenly there was a beep sound. "Someone's calling you Richie."

"Yeah... it's your dad."

"Keep me on a call conference call him back."

"Okay... just a second..."

Her father picked up in one ring. "Richie, you are supposed to come with your friend Reigh for investigation in this bloody case in front of Chris' house."

THREE
THE GUARD

Reigh was constantly trying to reach Seren's phone but it was unreachable.

"No use, huh?" a person said behind him.

"No," he replied. "And YOU are supposed to do something and here I AM doing everything."

"You sure she can and she will help you?"

"She will never betray me and ALWAYS help me. ALWAYS."

"Okay gotcha. But if we get caught..."

"Don't even think of it," Reigh said.

He rang again, with no use.

***

Richie grabbed his cycle, pedalling furiously with as much force as he can.

Towards the Mayor's house.

Seren paced her room up and down. They all were stuck, and somehow her dad too.

"Please be safe, Seren and Reigh," he thought, cycling at a huge pace towards Chris' house. "'cause I am not."

Richie turned the corner and Reigh passed the opposite street behind him without looking at him.

Seren found the use of her binoculars the second time that way.

She tried to look for any of the three people on the streets. She didn't see anyone at first, but then she noticed someone moving on the streets with a black hoodie.

Her first thought: Reigh.

Her second thought: Chris' murderer.

Her third thought: The... or her father.

Then finally that guy removed his hoodie and moved straight on.

The guard.

She grabbed her phone and rung Richie. "Pick up pick up..." she muttered.

Finally, he picked it up, "I know you are worried Seren but..."

"The guard is in Bridge-street A block. With a hoodie."

"Wearing a hoodie is not a crime."

"But what is he doing there? Also, he has a scar on his face..."

"SO? CHRIS HAS GONE MISSING! AND MY OTHER FRIEND IS CURRENTLY THE MOST WANTED CRIMINAL!"

"Richie turn the next right NOW!"

"I don't care. Now you just..." he froze. Seren also saw it. She held her breath. The guard was on his right, only about 15 meters away.

And Reigh was on his left, about one half a football far off.

And the guard held a gun pointing towards them.

Richie wasn't able to breathe.

"You cannot kill me," Reigh said. "Neither my friend."

"Why?"

"You don't know do you?"

"What?"

"The key to finding the cube is with me, and the location of the lock is known by Richie," he said confidently.

He's mad, Seren thought biting her lips, to keep from laughing. Then she shook her head. *Be serious,* she told herself.

"What?" the guard asked, mystified.

"You heard me."

"I can still torture you two," he said.

"Oh yeah? We are children. One bullet is enough to kill us, no matter where it strikes."

"There are other means too."

"We are still free and we have 21 gears cycles. Also, I have something you don't."

He looked straight into his eye with firm determination. He stared harder...

"I have a proper and nice... really nice and brilliantly foolishly insane... brain."

What next happened was really unbelievable.

There was no Richie firstly.

Richie was never there completely in their midst. He hadn't come completely on the road. Reigh's starring competition was just a trick.

Secondly, the guard had lowered his gun.

And thirdly, Reigh was perfectly in range with the guard. He was close enough that if he threw a stone, it will easily meet its target.

And fourthly, he was holding a really nice hard stone.

And then he threw it, and it met its target.

Reigh always wanted to see how it felt to crack someone's skull with a stone. And he saw it that day. The stone broke the guard's nose and blinded his one eye, and it also gave him a huge gash at his head with a lot of swelling.

Reigh juggled one more stone.

"You were warned," the guard said.

"Run," Reigh said.

The guard lifted his gun. Reigh smiled. "Shoot," he said.

And the guard didn't hesitate.

The bullet flew straight and met its target.

Richie.

He was peeping to see what was going on, with his left hand too vulnerable.

He spun and fell to the ground. He didn't feel anything. He just knew that he was almost dead. Then came the pain.

He had read in a few books, *I felt relieved when I felt the pain since it told me I was alive.*

Richie now had to admit, the hardest and the least paid attention to part was to be paralyzed with pain.

Reigh ran towards him and knelt beside him. He took out Richie's phone and rang someone.

Richie made a weak try to raise his hand, but he was successful in saying one word- "Don't."

Reigh rang his mother.

Then he kept Richie's phone in his inner pocket. "Help is on its way. Just... faint."

Richie was grateful to get the permission.

Reigh ran after picking up a few stones.

This time, the guard will repay. Reigh will repay the pullet with ten times sized stones.

He ran.

Then suddenly his phone rang..

"I am guiding you," Seren said.

"Seren?" Reigh said, relieved. "I have been calling you... since this madness started. These bad people have cloned my NUMBER."

"That's why my father turned pale when you called. Still, I am really relieved to speak to you. How long has this been going on?"

"Ten O'clock. When I received that stupid call."

"Reigh," she said, sounding really worried, "You fine?"

"No."

"I can understand..."

"No I mean that guy just disappeared. I was trying to corner him."

"Where are you?"

"Three streets north to your house. I guess he has gone further north."

Reigh went and somehow managed to climb the wall with the help of a pole and then he stepped to the railing and jumped the other side. Then he ran again through a garden, destroying the flowers perfectly.

"I am calling my friend. She can help us."

"*Me.* You are not in this and I prefer you to be safe."

"Why?"

"Because... because I care about you. And this is *my* mess. My stupid keys."

"We are in this together, Reigh. And no-nos et Cetra. We are in this together, and that's because you cannot do anything without me."

"I can do a lot of things!" he complained.

"We have the same reason for helping each other."

"This is my mess," he said.

"The line that you said before it."

He smiled. "Call your friend."

***

Iris was trying *real* hard to contact Chris, but it seemed useless.

"Come on," she said to herself, "A guy who is kidnapped and most probably murdered also isn't gonna pick up your call."

She kept her cell down and started tapping on her table as she rested her shoulders on the chair behind her.

By the way, I think I should introduce her. Iris was the student head of her school's own (kind of) newspaper. Kind of because it was only interesting for school children and contained only news related to school (duh) and obviously, it had a pretty boring *fixed* layout (though the students weren't able to understand the need for a 'fixed' layout).

But getting kidnapped by her classmate by her *another* classmate was on another level of hell and making a report of it or finding him was no less than finding the hell itself.

So that's why she was trying to connect to him.

And then there was news about Reigh too...

'*It has been reported that Reigh Whitten has gone missing!*'

Obviously, there are only three people who will know about him:

His family. And they do not have a clue.

Richie and Chris, his best friends. And now Chris is gone.

Hmm. Interesting. What if he killed Chris and ran away.

Ugh, too wild a theory.

Then Seren. Iris was pretty sure that she did know where he was, just she was hiding.

But why?

And then, there was another news...

The breaking in into the Grande Hall.

She may have very little idea about her classmates, but she was ready to bet it had to be Reigh. She was able to see it because of the neatness with which it was done.

But what exactly was Reigh trying to do?

She had even tried his number but it was all in vain.

She was looking at her pretty much empty flowchart, whose focus has somehow automatically shifted from Chris to Reigh.

She rang a new number, this time hoping to get some news.

And the phone of Seren was busy.

"Who the hell is she talking to *now*?"

Her mother opened the door from behind her and came in.

"Oh my god, I cannot believe it. Iris, you are awake!"

"Mom," she said, turning, "No school today."

"Sick or holiday?"

"Both."

"Great. But if you are sick, I would recommend the bed."

"No thanks. I have slept long enough."

Her mother shrugged, went out and closed the door.

She wrote a name on her whiteboard and started to look again at the jotted points. She turned on her laptop and typed Grande Hall.

***

"See, I am telling you about what I see. This is ALL I see. There is no one running," Seren's friend said.

"Okay, thanks," she kept her call.

"No use," Reigh said, who was there on the conference.

Seren sighed, "I guess I need to use the last retort."

"You don't. Because I saw him," he said. "The man is on a bike."

In the heavy mist, slowly by the bushy corner of someone's house, he peeked out and narrowed his eyes to see.

When he was able to figure out the scene, he hid back, his eyes wide and heart thumping at least a thousand times faster than any normal human heart.

***

The guard fired his first shot, his gun pointing straight to the head of his target.

FOUR

New Piece

Iris almost fainted as she yelled and got down (got down is generous). The glass has shattered in one shot, but it only had the strength to shatter the glass.

Her phone rang. It was Seren.

"How can your timing be so perfect," she said, breathing heavily.

"That guy is trying to cross your fence!" Someone yelled on the phone.

And she was pretty sure it was not Seren.

Neither was it, Reigh.

Nor any of her friends she knew.

"See," the voice said, "As long as you listen you are safe."

Now, it was either her dream or her ear was ringing due to the sound of the gunshot.

"Seren, you think that you will use voice changer and change your voice to Alien type to fool me?" Iris said on the phone.

"You got a bit too deep, didn't you?" someone said behind her.

She turned and gasped.

The guard was on the ledge of her window, gun pointing towards her.

She yelled as the guard reached out for the trigger...

And then...

He yelled and fell.

“If I were you I would have already run and hidden behind my mom,” Reigh’s voice said over the phone. “But I always do stupidity at the wrong moments, don’t I?”

"What the *hell* are you doing, Reigh?" Seren said, this time in a normal voice.

Iris heard three shots outside her house.

But Reigh stood right in front of the guard, unarmed.

And the guard had a nice pistol typo gun (she did not play shooting games to know the name of each and every gun unlike all the boys of her school).

But, he knew one thing, that the guard has not come to kill him. He had come to kill Iris.

Because she had too much information. That has to be it. Reigh was sure.

She knew something, knowingly or unknowingly, that makes a complete picture.

Or at least a clear picture.

“Why do you want to kill her?”

“She is a piece. And I cannot let all of them come together.”

“Firstly, we are not part of some sort of game. Secondly, all I want is to get out of this mess. Thirdly, I have a question. If you do not want the pieces to come together, why not kill me?”

“You have the cube. As soon as you give it to us, we will leave this country. Story finished. You live your life, we live ours.”

"Firstly, I do not have the cube. Secondly, you cannot kill me, right? So you cannot kill Iris."

He chuckled. "Your reusing your old trick is funny."

He smiled. "You think I am using my 'old trick'?"

"Yup."

"Then who are you waiting for? You have your gun. Fire at her." Reigh pointed at one of the windows where she was watching from. "Or you only have bullets for show." Then as silently as possible, he said, "Only move back. Run only on my cue."

"I hope I will not die," She said.

"Fire!" he yelled at the guard.

"You are so foolish," the guard said and fired. "You think that if I kill her then I will get the blame. Then, let me tell you, I won't."

Reigh gasped, "How did you..." He lunged forward.

But the guard had already fired.

Iris knew she was going to die the next second.

The glass broke.

And Iris stood there unharmed.

Reigh laughed and almost fell down laughing.

The guard raised his gun again, and Iris. Then, still smiling, he pressed the trigger.

Nothing happened.

"Firstly, the glass used in her home has the netted windows at that part behind the glass, which was clearly visible behind it. Secondly, most of the pistols have only 6 bullets," he said, slowly edging towards his bicycle.

She tossed Reigh a lighter and ran back inside.

Reigh ran towards his bicycle. The guard ran towards his bike. Reigh immediately sat on it and cycled as fast as possible. The Guard's bike was considerably farther. He cycled towards it and grabbed his bike as fast as possible and opened the fuel tank.

His observant eyes have easily spotted that the key was still on his bike, not even removed from the ignition.

The guard's jaw hung open, as Reigh, with a smile, tossed the burning lighter in.

***

Richie hated being stuck at the hospital.

But unfortunately, he had no choice.

A doctor came in, with a nurse behind him. "You do not need anything to sleep or some painkiller, do you?"

"No, I do not. Thanks. All I want is to call someone," Richie replied.

The Nurse started changing the IV bottle.

"Your parents are not too happy about the police stuff, you know."

"Anything new?"

"Oh, c'mon, don't be so rude," the doctor said. "But, by the way, there is something new. The chief thinks you are involved in the breaking in of the Mayor's house."

"He does?" Richie asked, trying to act surprised.

"Well, yes. But they need confirmation."

He laughed, "And they think that if they catch a criminal, he's going to confirm that he is the criminal."

The Nurse turned on the flow of the liquid in the plastic bottle.

"That depends on the conditions. How are you feeling Richie?"

"Conditions?" He turned and fainted.

But he read the words 'NARCO' written in bold on the plastic bottle before fainting.

***

"How long do I have?" Chief asked.

"He's a kid. Max to max 20 minutes. Then we will have to disconnect it," Doctor Clair answered.

"That's defined medical standards? Or..."

"Actually he can hold it for 30 minutes from the time we start. I just need to signal the nurse, but according to the rules...."

Chief slid an expensive phone in his pocket.

"Seriously?" the doctor asked. "This is nothing for me."

"Cloned numbers. Each number, if you sell, will cost millions. You just need to find potent buyers."

"How do I believe you?"

The chief looked at his expensive smartwatch. "Doctor I have 38 charges already against you, you know?"

Clair forgot how to breathe. 38 attempts, all successful and well planned has bought him millions of dollars. And all of them...

"On my phone," His thoughts left his mouth in form of words.

Chief scoffed. "I have more power than you can think of, doctor."

"You have thirty minutes," Richard said, turning pale, "Tell me when to start."

"Now."

He signalled. The chief opened the door and went in.

***

"We need to find the cube," Reigh said.

"See, your code needs to be something that she can understand," Iris told him.

They were in Iris' garage, whose back part was being currently used by Reigh and Iris to brainstorm ideas.

"The limit," Reigh said, "She said that the guard limit has been removed."

"I have a silly idea," Iris said, "But it's silly."

"Yeah?"

She took a deep breath, "Listen..."

***

Seren picked up Iris' call the next day at 12 in the afternoon, "Yeah?"

"Seren, can you help me with a maths question?"

"Yeah?"

"You may need your notebook with your pen kept at your table and trust me, this will leave you brainstorming for 12 hours from now."

"I am always asleep at 12 O'clock."

"Solve this question then, a triangle HGI has two points, E and R respectively, on its exterior and interior. Ugh, sorry, no not this one. This one: A person needs your help to find the surface area of a colourless 6 coloured cube kept inside a rectangular plot such that the walls of the plot are fenced and restrict entry..."

"This question does not make any sense. Even if it did, then my brain isn't working."

"Oh, sorry actually I... I just got mixed up in questions. Umm, I am sorry. No problem, I will ask my teacher."

Seren cut the call.

And smiled.

HGIER needs your help to find a colourless Rubik's cube inside a fenced rectangular plot.

REIGH needs your help to find a colourless Rubik's cube inside a fenced rectangular plot.

Lame try, but she guessed that no one would have interpreted it this way.

***

"I am pretty sure your plan would have worked," Reigh said. Iris knew that if it would have been anyone else then that person would have scoffed or laughed at her. But Reigh was very much different.

"I am really feeling dumb, unable to do anything," she said. "I am just... sitting and watching the show as my friends get in horrible danger!"

"You know what, Seren also have this type of nature. And that's what makes you two special."

"Your always cool mind is what makes you the best in school, but tell me, are you still not like... in a fix? Isn't your brain in an exploding condition?"

He laughed. "Firstly, I am not the best. Secondly, see... having a cool mind in the toughest situation allows me to think. So I never lose it."

"You are not confused?"

"I am in a horrible mess, and I do not have info," he said spreading his hands, "But I am not confused."

"How, exactly?"

"I know what to do. And I will do that only. It's much better than sitting and scratching your head."

"I disagree."

"None of my concern. By the way, you are a piece. So what do you know?"

"Kinda rude," she said, "The mayor died due to a genetic disease and the person who contacted you was a genetic scientist."

"I know."

"Okay."

"You knew something else before that person attacked you."

"I am sorry?"

He sighed. "You know something else too. And I *know* you are hiding."

She exhaled. "My sim was blocked three days ago. That's why I was using my dad's number. Others whose sims were blocked went away with a casual shrug, but I traced it down. I was the closest to this mystery, thanks to my junior journalist ID."

"It works?" Reigh asked with a raised eyebrow.

"I do. Even I was shocked at first, it did work. Well, I breached a nice firewall of that company's data..."

"How?" Reigh asked.

"My dad's an engineer."

"And he helped you?"

"Obviously."

"Okay. Go on."

"So well, I found there was a dual-route from and to my number. That meant it was cloned, and my sim was really poking its nose in the cloned business."

"Okay. Makes a bit sense."

"But that was not the end of it. My sim was blocked by the company itself."

"Hmm."

"So I tried to contact the CEO to warn him... but then things started going wrong."

"Doesn't make sense."

"It doesn't?"

"Why randomly block a few numbers when you get a hell lot of fake sims?"

"Okay. And?"

"Why did they not block my sim?"

"If you did not want me to speak to or to contact anyone, and you have the option of making a dual way such that you are going to receive any call directed to that person..."

"Makes sense."

"And for your first question... it was not a random bunch of numbers."

"It was not random?"

"Pseudorandom you can say. Seemingly random."

"Okay. How?"

Iris stood up and walked up to her desk. She took out a file from a locker in her Mahogany table and handed Reigh a sheet of paper.

"You know half the people in this list."

"Hmm... Maybe..." He stopped. "My parents, classmates... oh no, no, no..."

"This is not all," she handed him a bunch of papers.

It had sound wave plots of the same 38 people, from their calls.

"When did you get these?" Reigh asked.

"The exact second after these were blocked," she hesitated.

"And?"

"The exact moment after you received that call."

FIVE

RUNAWAY

Richie hated being stuck at the hospital, but he did not have much choice.

Still, he was constantly looking at the window, sulking and wondering what all he had given away. His heart was throbbing pretty badly, and he felt sick.

But the strangest thing was yet to happen.

The door opened, and a nurse came in. This time she was without the doctor.

"Richie," she said, "How can we get we get you out of here?"

He narrowed his eyes.

She exhaled and took off her cap and mask. Richie's jaw hung open.

Putting this all in Reigh's style, firstly, she was about the same age as that of Richie.

Secondly, she was just *Gorgeous.*

And thirdly, strangers of such an age helping in hospitals while hiding their faces like criminals cannot be good.

But what would Chris say?

As long she is getting you out, get out.

He decided to follow Chris.

"Who arc you?"

"Venice," she said. "But I live in New York."

"And why exactly are you getting me out?"

"I am a detective."

"No offence, but... pretty young for that, huh?"

"Typical. I thought every teen in the whole Boston area was more knowledgeable than the teens in New York."

"What does this has to do with it?"

She smiled, "You mean business, don't you?"

"I... do...n't."

"Okay."

"Fine. Come to the point."

"So this is the plan, I get you some nice clothes, you get to the storeroom where all the cleaning stuff is, then just open a window where you can easily reach. And then, there are no bars there. Just jump. I will send them on your trail. They will run behind you, lose you, and by that time you will be injured on a stretcher and you will be taken to the operation theatre. There we will jump and we will get away."

"But why such a lot of trouble? You are new to the city I guess?"

"I am not here to stay. I am here to investigate. And I will *not* leave without doing what I have in my mind. I am saving you because you were in this hospital and I got your NARCO records. But they are stuck. I swapped the fake one with the original one."

"WHAT?!" Richie exclaimed. "THEN *I* AM STUCK!!"

"I did not have much choice," she said with a casual shrug. "You coming or not?" She offered her hand.

"You really did not leave me much choice," he said taking it.

***

Richie hated his disguise.

But now it was time to change.

He has somehow, hiding from the public eye, made it to the storeroom in a Janitor's coat and mask. And now, from a Janitor's uniform, he was shifting into a patient's one, fresh from the laundry.

Just it has been taken from the bunch of clothes that were waiting to be laundered in the laundry.

Great. Just great.

The shirt had bloodstains. Still, closing his nose, he wore them. Then he jumped.

The rest of their plan went accordingly. They reached their destiny, opened the window, and then stopped.

No way, Richie thought, *This girl needs to be Frankenstein in order to* think *of such an idea.*

She laughed. "I am not *that* mean to make you jump from here."

They were 17 stories up *at least.*

"Then how?" he asked.

"I guess I should warn you," she said, "Not many people trust me."

He scoffed. "I am no better."

She climbed the window, and then hung her legs. Then with one swift move, she swung herself inside the window below them.

"Okay," Richie said to himself, "I cannot be serious about following that girl."

But still, reluctantly, fighting all his fears he hung his legs and jumped.

For one horrific moment, he felt he was going to die.

But when he made it, it just felt like a moment.

He was in a yellow room, only lit by a single window which they have broken. The door was slightly open, and there were racks and rows of CDs and stuff everywhere. This part of the hospital seemed more like a movie rent library than a part of a hospital.

"That was the most daring stunt I have ever done," Venice said. "What about you?"

"I have been shot by a real bullet."

"Okay," she said with a laugh. "But it was just a... okay I know how it feels. I won't comment."

"You too have been shot?"

"Once. Thrice I have been fired at."

"Scary," he said with a shudder.

"Change now. We are in the storage room. Now it's gonna be easy."

"Uh... now?"

"Do not tell me you left your clothes back," she said.

"Well, just a silly mistake... umm... I didn't have normal clothes. They were taken as soon as I was admitted."

She rolled her eyes. "I gave you a laundry bag."

"Yeah, it's still with me."

"Check it."

He checked it and saw that there were his clothes, neatly laundered and folded.

"Okay got it."

"I am just going out. I need some... things. You get ready within exactly two minutes. Lock the door from inside." She knocked on the wall... in a pattern. Three fast and two with a pause. "Open only when you hear this."

"Got it."

"Good," she left the room. He slipped on his clothes as there was knocking on the wooden door. He opened the door.

Richie tried to hold his jaw in place. She had a yellow packet, with a few injections. She had changed too. She wore a brown jacket with a fur hood on a black top with grey jeans. She had brown eyes, jet black hair and an expensive smartwatch on her hand.

"You... changed the colour of your hair?"

"I wore a wig at that time," she told him with a casual shrug. "Helps with disguises, you know."

"Okay... So what now?"

"I don't have any special attachment to this place. So let's get out. I have information, you have information. We exchange... if getting you out isn't enough."

"Then we part ways?" he asked, trying not to sound as disappointed as he felt.

She shrugged. "Depends. From what I know, I don't think that the end of this story is near. So most probably: no."

"Okay. So let's get out."

"So here are the rules, AVOID the elevator. WALK confidently. And when I suddenly turn at you and speak proper rubbish, you REPLY to it CONFIDENTLY WITHOUT LOOKING SKEPTICAL. Understood?"

"Umm... maybe. Yes."

"Let's go then. And also, you are FOLLOWING ME and you are my best friend and we have come to see my aunt, Mrs Whitten, admitted on bed 112 in the OPD. Also, I own a white SUV with number 1297."

"Okay. I'll... try to remember."

"Good. Let's go now."

They went into the corridor as fast and casually as possible.

Suddenly Richie saw the doctor who gave him the NARCO. Probably Venice also saw it, because she held his hand and blocked the doctor's view towards Richie.

"You know what, Simon," she said holding his hand and locking her eyes with his, "My aunt said that you drive *real* rough."

"That, I *actually* do."

"But she didn't even see you drive," she complained. Her tone seemed so natural that he was stunned. It was as if she has practised it a thousand times. Her tone seemed irritated and influenced with a childish frustration, that made him look at her in a very different way.

"Maybe she guessed," he said with a shrug.

"Still..."

He threw his hands up, "I am giving up."

She left eye contact, looked around her and chuckled. "We left that doctor *way* behind us and I was so mesmerized I didn't even notice."

He smiled, "Neither did I." Then he noticed that they had even started climbing down the stairs. She hasn't yet left his hand. "You know what? I have never *ever* run away like a culprit before. I usually leave the culprit work to Reigh and Chris."

She laughed softly again. "You are really *really* bad at lying."

"I am?"

"I *know* what you did, Richie."

"Well, truthfully I did not do anything."

"Who distracted the police chief while his *own* daughter helped two people break into the Grande hall?"

His jaw hung open, "How did you..."

"I know what you were doing. But do *you* know why I came before you? From New York city?"

It dawned on him. "You were threatened."

She nodded. "When I was coming here I saw the strangest thing: Reigh was accused of *murder* and theft. But the common thing? The guard who died had *no* idea that Reigh was the thief. And the guard died from a dagger, whereas none was available in your town of that kind. And the police has issued the statement of Reigh going *missing* to the media, and they haven't told them the charges. That's not all... your friend Chris who was supposedly dead still has his phone *switched on*. If the police was have a proper investigation, they would have his phone. Which they don't. Chris is alive. His phone was taken by the police but now they do not have it. Also, the police know Chris was the one who went in. Then why are they accusing Reigh? And... yes! The common thing. They found two blood samples, and one of them is much more than the other. The strangest thing is that the prominent one is not of Chris. It's unnaturally more, and it's of a person suffering from haemophilia... and CIPA. That's what the gene lab report says. And the guard also has both. And they both are super rare. But those blood samples are not completely the same."

"I guess... you know a hell lot of things."

"That I do," she said with a smile. "And... I also know where Chris is."

His jaw hung open. "How...?"

"The only mistake the police did," she said, "Was to not look for his *other* phone using the mobile signal satellite. They seem to be trying to keep this matter as low as possible. And that's... *not* good."

He noticed that they have reached her car. She left his hand and handed him the keys. "My mother does not allow me to drive rough, and right now we have to."

He took the keys. "You don't know what you are asking for."

"The information?"

He chuckled, "No, the car."

She rolled her eyes. "Just drive."

He got in a pulled out of the parking. It was a white SUV, neatly cleaned, well kept with an air freshener and a full HD small-sized screen.

He pressed down the brake as hard as he could when he got on the road. He completely pressed the accelerator, and then finally released the break. Venice was thrown back against her seat. She spent the rest of the way screaming, but it took Richie only five minutes to reach his cousin's house.

"What place is this?" she asked.

"Somewhere safe. Come in." He opened the front door and walked in. He rang the bell. His cousin came to the door.

Her eyes narrowed as she opened the door. "Who is she?" she asked Richie.

"A friend of mine. She saved me from the hospital."

"Oh... so after you get shot you need to be saved from the hospital too?"

Richie's jaw hung open. "How did you know?"

"Iris? Who's there?" Her father asked.

"It's Richie, dad. And his friend. You two better come in. Reigh is not in the house. Things have gone a few trillion hells lot more than the worst that could be possible, you know."

SIX

STRANGE MESSAGES

Seren wasn't sure what was going on.

A permanent guard has been positioned in front of her door. The CCTV outside has been repositioned such that it had the best view of the door.

Her father has raised the crisis to the family level. But the question is, why?

Maybe Reigh said something stupid during the call. Maybe her father interpreted a joke seriously. Literally, anything is possible.

Seren rested her elbows on the window frame. Looking out she saw the place where it all started. Looking carefully, she focused on the Grande Hall, trying to get all the missed info.

The snow has melted a bit, but still, in the snow the grass was green. This was due to the transparent polycarbonate sheet joining the fence to the edges of the roof, beyond which was a rooftop garden. The house was very well maintained, with the courtyard facing sliding door open. There were no officers investigating at that point of time.

Seren took her trustworthy binoculars from her shelf and looked at them fondly. It had been a gift from Reigh two years ago.

"It will help you when it's not that you cannot trust anyone, but instead when you just don't want to trust anyone. It will show you what your eyes cannot."

These were his words that day. And this was the best gift Reigh has ever managed. Usually, he sticks to giving something new, innovative and surprising, but of course, he usually fails.

Keeping the fond memories aside she went to the window and looked straight at the Grande Hall.

"Seren?" Someone called behind her.

"Yeah?" she turned hastily.

"What happened?" It was her mom. She was about forty years old, with a beautiful face and brown hair. Everyone said that the looks that make Seren famous have been gifted to her by her mother.

"What do you mean?"

"What's with the binoculars?"

"I was just, you know, trying to sight some nice birds."

"See, I know you are worried about Reigh. But I know him and your dad. It's gonna be perfectly fine."

"And what exactly is with the security?"

"That's what I wish to speak with you about."

"Go on."

Her mother rolled her eyes.

"Come in Mom and close the door," Seren said.

"Great," she said as she went in and sat on Seren's bed.

"What were you saying?"

"The reason why your dad has established these guards make no sense to me. Neither did what Reigh seems to be signalling. At for a while."

Seren's jaw hung open. "He spoke about it to you?"

"What sort of game are you all playing, huh?"

"It's no game Mom, it's happening."

"I know that."

"I am sorry, *What?*"

She sighed. "Reigh is much smarter than you think. I have to get you out of this room."

"How so?"

"Just you need to use the washroom."

"Okay. That's it?"

Her mother shrugged, "I don't know."

She looked at the door.

Then she remembered.

The time... was 11:59.

It will leave you brainstorming for 12 hours...

"Mom," Seren asked, "When did you meet Reigh?"

"That's the thing. I never met him."

"Then... how?"

"I'll show you a picture," She took out her phone and showed her the image.

Her jaw hung open.

Always keep your mind and eyes open. You can need it any second.

In the kitchen, there was a small knife lying on the table. Its tip pointed to a mug with Seren's name which was a gift by her father, and its hilt towards an open faucet with a human figurine getting wet. Beside it was another mug kept upside down with a canvas on top of it which hung in the guest's room. It was the painting of a 'moor,' or so it said.

Bath-moor.

Opposite Mug.

Bath...room.

***

Seren somehow managed to go to the bathroom looking normal. Her mother has helped her too.

Just her mother did not know the mistake she has done... giving such a thing to Seren, and knowing that she *cannot* use it.

Seren half-knew what to expect. Another clue. Reigh did not like to stick to a single level of security.

She opened the door and entered.

Her washroom was like any other, a washbasin, a commode a shower and a bathtub. She guessed what all secrets could have Reigh hidden behind a single wooden door and in midst of a completely white tiled washroom.

She stepped in within the threshold. Then, without looking, she stepped on a soap, sliding and almost falling.

Almost.

Suddenly Reigh was there, his hand around her waist and pulling her up. They ended up in an awkward position with Reigh's hand around her waist, Seren's hands on his chest, and their eyes locked.

In Seren's eyes, Reigh was pretty much the same, with crystal blue mesmerizing eyes, brown hair and a perfect face figure. The reason why he was not completely the same was a small gash at his forehead, which would have spoiled anyone's looks (except Reigh, the cut only made him look cooler), still bled. He wore faded jeans with a dark green hoodie.

And as for Seren, in the simplest words, she still looked awesome. She also had brown lustrous hair and brown eyes. She was wearing a pair of vibrant blue jeans and a T-shirt, not at all bothered by the cold.

He awkwardly let go of her, both of them looking here and there for a second and then finally looking up.

"You interpreted my message?" he asked.

"Truthfully, my mom did," she admitted.

He chuckled, "Now I'll have to think twice before leaving symbolic messages."

"You'd better. By the way, from what I got of Iris' message, I need to help you find a cube?"

He grinned, "Never thought you would have interpreted."

"I can do a lot more than you think I am capable of."

"Great. So here's my escape plan," he said. Then he started thinking.

"How exactly did you get in?"

"That's one mystery I leave to you for solving. By the way, where are your car keys?"

Why the hell did mom give it to me? She held out the keys. "My mom expects you take the older one and not even get a scratch on it."

He chuckled. "Then she never would have given the new car keys. It's up to me, I guess."

She sighed. "So it seems."

***

Getting to the car part was the easiest. Seren just had to open the door, make the fresh air excuse and walk out. But Reigh was about to have difficulties.

He sent a text message to Iris.

And the very next second she saw the message, the lights went out.

Just great.

He sent another text message, this time to Seren herself. Flicking the mains MCB off, the leftover inverter powered lights went out.

Then, unseen to everyone, he walked out.

What Iris did was simple, she made Richie destroy the main transformer by cutting the main power lines using a simple but efficient technology: An exceptionally heavy arrow with a saw kind of thing attached.

And the saw was capable of cutting hard metal barrier wires.

Then they hooked the arrow to Venice's car and drove off, cutting the wire.

As simple as that.

And now, without being noticed, Reigh walked out straight through the main corridor.

A thief cannot steal in broad daylight, so he first waits for it to end...

...or he himself steals the daylight.

***

Seren and Reigh stood in front of the garage and started unlocking the main door. While Reigh was unlocking it, Seren stood back, watching. "I still am unable to guess how you got in."

He laughed. "Think harder," he said without looking at her. "Think like me."

Seren frowned. "Seriously, don't try to flatter yourself."

Reigh chuckled.

"By the way," Seren asked as Reigh got up, "Why are we taking a car? The Grande Hall is too close."

Reigh grinned. "Your guess is as good as mine."

"Wait for a second, what?"

"Guess."

"NO," Seren said, shaking her head. "I already am stuck in one mystery."

"Fine," he said, "We are leaving a bread crumb trail. Makes any sense?"

"Nope. Why do you want us arrested?"

"Not us. I leaving a trail to our destination."

Then it dawned on her. "You are leading the officers to the Grande hall."

"Exactly."

A perfect plan.

When Seren's sudden disappearance will be investigated, they will find the puzzle at the sink, the Soap Seren stepped upon and the missing car. They will trace her with the car's GPS... which will lead them straight to the hall. Not only will this remove the allegation of kidnapping Seren from Reigh's head but also it will cause an investigation in the hall, spilling out its mysteries.

"Wise," she admitted.

"Get in the car," Reigh said, opening the shotgun door for her.

"I am driving," she said.

"No, you are not. We need to leave an unmistakable trail."

That brought a kind-of glint in her eyes. "What's the plan for that?"

"Firstly we need to make your car easily recognizable."

"And how will you do that?" Her green Chevrolet Camaro clearly stood out like a sore thumb. But still, Seren was still intrigued to hear his plan...

"By not getting even a single scratch on it."

She rolled her eyes, "Seriou... hey, wait!" Reigh had turned on the car and the front lights were blinding her.

He blared the horns. "Come in before the officers come out."

She rolled her eyes but got into the car. The talk-occupying trick of Reigh was actually paying off.

Reigh blared the horn very hard again and drove off into the lane.

Seren thought about telling what she saw while looking through her binoculars, but she knew that what she saw was not possible. It could not have been true. After all, she only 'glimpsed' it for a second before her mother came in.

The only thing that she did not know was that the fact she was not speaking was actually one of the two pieces of information that she carried, and will continue to carry. This piece of information will bring her the closest possible to her demise in very recent times.

But right now, the only known players are the ones who don't know the enemy.

And the enemy had the pieces on gun tip.

Epilouge

The current inhabitants of the grande hall were currently on full surveillance mode. The order had come only 12 hours ago.

Kill them all the second you see them.

A yellow Camaro appeared in front of the gate.

"How much time will it take to blow them with a volley of shots?" the head of the operation asked.

"Depends upon how many guns we will be using," one of the senior operating agents answered.

"How many do we have at our disposal?"

The agent looked at him, "700 AK-47 and about 400 different types of handguns."

"How many men?"

"900 or so."

Without even a touch of emotion on the face of the head of the operation on killing two partially innocent people, he said two lines, "Blow them with all men firing with the fastest speed possible. Make them unrecognizable."

Then without even the slightest hesitations, guns were in the arms of men, and then they all broke loose.

If only Seren would have told Reigh what she has seen, Richard's archer friend could have had been saved.

***

Horrified, Kate stayed hidden behind a pillar. She has seen the shots destroying the car. Her only hope was catching Seren's eye and using her help to escape.

But now, it seemed she was dead.

Printed by Libri Plureos GmbH in Hamburg, Germany